ADVENTURES WITH · Invisibles
HIDDEN PICTURE FUNBOOK

WRITTEN & ILLUSTRATED BY
LARRY EVANS

(FORMERLY *INVISIBLES 1*)

ISBN: 0-8431-3884-X   First Revised Edition   10 9 8 7 6 5 4 3 2 1

TROUBADOR PRESS
an imprint of
PRICE STERN SLOAN
Los Angeles

IN-VISIBLE 1

PIRATE CHASE

The square rigged clipper ship is outrunning the pirate ship by using all her sails. Hidden on board are an anchor, a ship's wheel, oar, dinghy, telescope, pirate sword *and* a rotten old pirate.

IN-VISIBLE 2

GIANT'S CASTLE

This magnificent castle belongs to a giant named Ralph. He doesn't like visitors so he is hiding. If *you* can find him, ask him how the weather is up there. He will think that is funny and give you a *big hug*.

IN-VISIBLE 3

THE FOXY FOX

The fox from the cover of this book is being chased by a horse and rider and three hounds. The fox thinks he's really clever, but they're *all* right there in the picture with him. I think this fox has his goose cooked!

IN-VISIBLE 4

A HOT SUMMER DAY

All the people have gone to the beach and left the cat home. But a surfer along with two girls in bathing suits, a sailboat and a guitar are there to keep it company.

IN-VISIBLE 5

LIGHTHOUSE

A wide variety of boats and ships have found their way upon this rocky shore: a Roman Trireme with its sails and oars, a Mississippi River boat, a Chinese Junk, an Ocean Liner and a Venetian Gondola. See if you can find them all.

IN-VISIBLE 6

CHECKERS

Uncle Jake and his friend Wilbur are retired, but the tools of their trade are there in the old country store with them. A saw, hammer, hatchet, pickaxe, screwdriver, and scissors are somewhere in the picture. They both were building contractors. The scissors were for cutting *red tape*.

IN-VISIBLE 7

STILL LIFE

The vase of flowers is ready for the artist to paint, but he is no where to be found. Find a paint brush, palette *and* the artist before the flowers wilt.

IN-VISIBLE 8
THE QUEEN

Her Royal Majesty is ready for the official portrait to be painted by our elusive artist from the last IN-VISIBLE. She wants her faithful dog to be in the painting but he is off chasing a rabbit. Find the rabbit, the dog, a hairbrush and the King somewhere in the picture.

IN-VISIBLE 9
THE HIDDEN JUNGLE

On pages 18 and 19 lies an illustration of the jungle watering hole. The Abongo natives *know* that the animals come here to drink, and the two tribesmen have been waiting for three days to capture an animal. The snake has been waiting three days for the *natives* to cross the old log. Hidden for the last three days right there in the picture are an elephant, rhino, giraffe, monkey, zebra, alligator, lion and antelope. See if you can find the animals *before* the natives capture them.

IN-VISIBLE 10

PREHISTORIC WALK

The hikers are taking a path that leads right into the age of Dinosaurs. Find the Apatosaurus, Pteranodon (flying Dinosaur) and the ferocious Tyrannosaurus Rex.

IN-VISIBLE 11

INDIAN HUNTER

The pioneers have driven all the animals into hiding. Running Bear is searching for a buffalo, big-horned sheep, beaver and a moose. They are all there in the picture with him along with the pioneer hunter who scared them away with his gun.

IN-VISIBLE 12

DAYDREAM

Mary Jane is daydreaming about the circus. She doesn't realize that the circus is right there in the picture with her. Find the elephant, lion, trapeze artist (on the trapeze), cotton candy, tightrope walker (on the tightrope, naturally), and three clowns. (No you silly, her clown doll doesn't count.)

IN-VISIBLE 13

THE BIRDS

Sally Ann swings in the giant sycamore tree every afternoon. When she swings all the birds disappear. Find eleven birds in the picture including an owl, a flamingo and a toucan. There is also a vulture, an egret, a gull, an eagle, a *tiny* duck, two birds trying to fly away and one bird just sitting there.

IN-VISIBLE 14

HAUNTED HOUSE

Nancy and her sister Elizabeth thought they would explore the old abandoned house on a warm summer's night. Suddenly lights appeared upstairs and weird noises echoed through the house. You see, the house is *really* haunted. Find the skull, owl, bat, ghost, spider, black cat and the old witch hidden in the picture.

SOLUTIONS

1

2

3

4

5

6

7

8

9

10

11

12

13

14

IMAGINATIVE *FUNBOOKS* FROM TROUBADOR PRESS

Adventures with Invisibles
Dinosaur Funbook
Gross and Gruesome Puzzles & Games
Imaginary Invisibles
Maze Craze 1
Maze Craze 2
Maze Craze 3
Nature's Treasures Invisibles
Oceans of Invisibles
3-D Mazes
Tough Mazes
Wild Wild West Puzzles & Games

*Also look for our Troubador Color & Story Albums, ColorPops,
and punch-out and assemble Action and Play Sets.*

Troubador Press books are available wherever books are sold or can be ordered directly from the publisher.
Customer Service Department
390 Murray Hill Parkway, East Rutherford, NJ 07073

 TROUBADOR PRESS
an imprint of
PRICE STERN SLOAN
Los Angeles